The Teen Guide to Adulting: Gaining Financial Independence

What You Need to Know About

MORTGAGES

JASON PORTERFIELD

New York

Published in 2021 by The Rosen Publishing Group, Inc.
29 East 21st Street, New York, NY 10010

Copyright © 2021 by The Rosen Publishing Group, Inc.

First Edition

All rights reserved. No part of this book may be reproduced in any form without permission in writing from the publisher, except by a reviewer.

Library of Congress Cataloging-in-Publication Data

Names: Porterfield, Jason, author.
Title: What you need to know about mortgages / Jason Porterfield.
Description: New York: Rosen Publishing, 2021 | Series: The teen guide to adulting: gaining financial independence | Audience: Grades 7–12. | Includes bibliographical references and index.
Identifiers: LCCN 2019013271| ISBN 9781725340633 (library bound) | ISBN 9781725340626 (pbk.)
Subjects: LCSH: Mortgages—Juvenile literature. | Mortgage loans—Juvenile literature.
Classification: LCC HG4655 .P67 2021 | DDC 332.7/2—dc23
LC record available at https://lccn.loc.gov/2019013271

Manufactured in China

CONTENTS

INTRODUCTION..4

CHAPTER ONE
MORTGAGE CRASH COURSE........................7

CHAPTER TWO
SOLID MORTGAGE FOUNDATIONS................18

CHAPTER THREE
A PERFECT MORTGAGE FIT......................29

CHAPTER FOUR
CLOSING TIME....................................42

CHAPTER FIVE
HOME FREE..55

GLOSSARY...66
FOR MORE INFORMATION.........................68
FOR FURTHER READING..........................72
BIBLIOGRAPHY.....................................74
INDEX..77

INTRODUCTION

After years of working and saving, you're finally ready to buy a home of your own. Many people see this as a major milestone and a mark of achievement. But are you as ready as you think you are?

You probably won't be able to afford to buy the home you want immediately. Buying a house or a condo (condominium) takes years of preparation and careful money management.

For many Americans, a home is the most expensive thing they will ever buy. Houses often cost hundreds of thousands of dollars. According to the Federal Reserve Bank of St. Louis, the average price of a house sold in the United States in February 2019 was $249,500. Condos often cost less, but can still be well above $100,000.

To cover the cost of a home, most buyers get a loan called a mortgage. A mortgage is a contract that a borrower signs with a lender to receive money for purchasing or renovating a home. The buyer pays the lender back in monthly payments over a set number of years until the loan is fully repaid. The buyer also pays the lender interest on the loan, which is a percentage of the loan amount that is added on to every payment. The lender can take possession of the home if the borrower falls behind on payments.

Getting a mortgage can be complicated. Homebuyers should take the time to find the lender that can provide them with the best interest rate possible. Banks, credit unions, and

Meeting with a mortgage broker is an important step for anyone who wants to buy a home. The broker can tell buyers about the types of loans that are available.

mortgage lending specialists are all possibilities a homebuyer should consider when shopping for a mortgage. The federal government also offers mortgages for some people, including low-income homebuyers, veterans, and farmers.

There's a lengthy application process involved in any mortgage. People have to show the lender that they have good credit, a steady income, and enough money saved to make a down payment. Financial advisers and lending professionals can help homebuyers through the mortgage process to receive the best rates possible. Keeping up with monthly payments for many years can seem like a burden, but the mortgage gives the borrower the opportunity to purchase and live in a home he or she otherwise could not afford in one payment.

Mortgages can be used to buy houses, condos, vacant land, and commercial buildings. A person who already owns property can get a mortgage to make improvements, such as building a new wing onto a house. Once the mortgage is paid, the property becomes the homebuyer's in full. He or she has full control of the property that is both a valuable asset and a place associated with many cherished memories.

CHAPTER ONE

1 MORTGAGE CRASH COURSE

It takes a great deal of money to buy a home. Whether it's a house or a condominium unit, a home is often the most expensive single thing a person purchases. Both houses and condos often cost tens of thousands of dollars or hundreds of thousands of dollars. The financial magazine *Kiplinger* stated in January 2019 that the median price of a house or condo in the 100 largest metropolitan areas in the United States was $240,000 at the end of December 2018. This number means that half of all homes sold in those cities cost more than $240,000 and half cost less.

That's a massive amount of money for most people, and few have that much saved up and ready to spend all at one time. Instead of paying the full price for the home at once, most homebuyers take out a mortgage that they will pay back over many years until they own the home outright. The lender pays the full amount to the seller, and the purchaser then repays the lender over that time.

Deciding that it's time to buy a home is a big step. Mortgage payments are often made on a monthly basis, so the homebuyer has to be sure to have enough money every month to cover

Homebuyers who take out a mortgage are responsible for making regular payments. Many people write a check every month to the lender until they have paid off their loan.

that cost or risk falling behind and paying more in the form of penalties. Figuring out whether you're ready for a mortgage should be an early part of the process of buying a home.

A COMPLEX LOAN

Although mortgages give the borrower the ability to make a purchase without having all the money needed at once, the borrower will ultimately pay more than the asking price. This situation is true even if the borrower makes all of his or her payments on time every month. Mortgages are structured in such a way that the institution lending the money makes a profit from the purchase.

Every mortgage is made up of several parts. The most important part to the borrower is the principal. This sum of money is the total amount being borrowed through the mortgage loan. The principal represents the money that is paid to meet the price asked by the seller.

Details of Amount Due/Paid

Principal and Interest	$1,579.78
Subsidy/Buydown	$0.00
Escrow	$472.87
Amount Past Due	$0.00
Outstanding Late Charges	$0.00
Other	$0.00
Total Amount Due	$2,052.65
Account Due Date	December 01, 2009

Mortgage bills are broken down so that borrowers can see how much of each check goes to pay the amount borrowed, as well as any other charges that might apply.

MORTGAGE CRASH COURSE

Interest is the money that goes to the lender. This extra money added onto the loan is to pay the lender for taking a risk by lending money out. It also compensates the lender for not being able to use the money for other purposes.

The interest a borrower has to pay is calculated according to an interest rate. The interest rate is a percentage of the loan principal. It is often called the annual percentage rate. Interest rates on mortgages have been very high at times, and very low at others. In the 1980s, interest rates sometimes rose higher than 15 percent on some mortgages, according to the Federal Home Loan Mortgage Corporation (FHLMC, also known as Freddie Mac). By 1991 they had fallen below 10 percent on average. In the early 2010s, after a major downturn in the housing market, they were consistently below 5 percent.

In addition to the actual cost of the home and the interest, the homebuyer may have to pay for insurance. Banks and lenders sometimes require their mortgage borrowers to purchase homeowners insurance. Homeowners insurance is an insurance policy that pays for damages in case of certain types of disasters. These policies may pay to help cover the cost of repairs needed in case of fires, landslides, earthquakes, and weather-related disasters such as tornadoes or blizzards. A homeowners insurance policy can also protect the homeowner in case of accidents that happen on his or her property or damages to another person's possessions. For example, a tree falling on a guest's car could be covered by some policies. However, the insurance becomes more expensive as it is used.

Homebuyers might be required to purchase private mortgage insurance (PMI). Private mortgage insurance is an insurance policy that works as a guarantee that the mortgage will be paid. These policies lower the risk to the lender. They are usually intended for people who otherwise would not qualify for a mortgage. By requiring them, banks and other lenders are lowering their financial risk. Mortgages from the Federal Housing Administration (FHA) and US Department of Agriculture often require the borrower to take out a mortgage insurance policy. According to the Consumer Finance Protection Bureau, homebuyers who make a down payment of less than 20 percent are often required to purchase a PMI policy before they can get a mortgage.

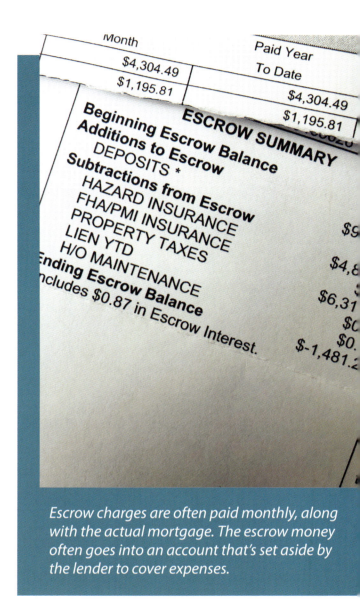

Escrow charges are often paid monthly, along with the actual mortgage. The escrow money often goes into an account that's set aside by the lender to cover expenses.

MORTGAGE CRASH COURSE

Many lenders have their mortgage borrowers make payments into an escrow account. An extra monthly charge is added to the mortgage bill. This money is used to cover expenses associated with the property the homeowner is buying, such as insurance costs and property taxes. Escrow payments are reassessed every year to make sure any increases in these expenses are covered.

A RATE DEBATE

Every mortgage has either a fixed or adjustable mortgage rate attached. With fixed-rate mortgages, the interest rate is set at a certain percentage of the loan amount and stays at that rate for the duration of the mortgage. A homebuyer who purchases a house with a mortgage that has a fixed, 4 percent rate will always pay that rate until the mortgage is paid off. Even if interest rates fall, that homebuyer is committed to paying 4 percent interest. Adjustable-rate mortgages (ARMs) change based on the current interest rates. If rates rise, the interest rate that a homebuyer with one of these mortgages pays also rises.

Fixed-rate and adjustable-rate mortgages both have advantages and drawbacks. Locking in a fixed-rate mortgage at a time when rates are very low can save money when rates get higher. ARMs can also be beneficial. They often start at rates that are lower than fixed-rate mortgages, giving homebuyers a chance to purchase homes that are more expensive than they might otherwise be able to afford. Their rates can also rise significantly over the life of the loan as interest rates go up. A loan officer or financial adviser can help borrowers decide which type of mortgage is right for them.

WHAT YOU NEED TO KNOW ABOUT MORTGAGES

WHY BUY?

The cost of paying a mortgage every month for a set number of years may make a person wonder what the point is in purchasing a home at all. In the United States, about two-thirds of the population owns a house, condo, or co-op unit, according to CityLab. The other 100 million people live in rental housing, whether it's a house, an apartment, or a rented room in a building shared with other renting tenants.

Younger people, especially those in their twenties, are more likely to rent. People with lower incomes also rent more often than people who make more money. In many cases, those two populations overlap. Many people in their twenties are only just starting their careers and might not make enough money to pay a mortgage.

In 2017, the US Census Bureau estimated that there were about 135.4 million total housing units across the country. That figure included single-family houses, condo units, and co-op housing. Of those homes, about 75.8 million were occupied by their owners. Renters lived in about forty-three million of those units.

Most of the homes that were occupied by their owners had a mortgage attached to them. About 41.8 million of those owner-occupied homes were mortgaged.

It can be more expensive in the short term to buy a home than to rent. A 2019 investigation by CNBC found that it was more expensive to own than to rent in every state at that time. In addition to the mortgage payment, homeowners have to pay for maintenance costs and cover expenses like property

Condos are smaller units, usually apartments, within larger buildings. First-time homebuyers may have an easier time getting a mortgage for a condo because they often cost less than houses.

taxes. However, their monthly costs go down significantly once the mortgage is paid off. They can also feel secure in knowing that they will never have to look for a new place to live because their landlord suddenly decided to increase their rent. Everything they pay toward their mortgage eventually goes to having full ownership of their home.

TERMS AND TIME FRAMES

The time frame in which a lender expects the borrower to pay off a mortgage is called a term. Mortgages have different loan terms. They are generally based on the amount that the borrower is able to pay every month. The amount of risk that the lender sees in the borrower can also be a factor in calculating the term of the mortgage and the interest rate. Borrowers who choose mortgages with shorter terms are seen by lenders as being at a lower risk to default (stop paying) on their mortgage. They may get a lower interest rate for the term than those who are judged to be riskier.

Mortgage payments are often made on a monthly basis, like utility or credit card bills. The borrower makes twelve monthly payments over a year. A biweekly mortgage requires a borrower to make payments every two weeks instead. These mortgages result in lower interest payments and a lower total cost of the home. However, they also require the borrower to be extremely vigilant in making those payments. Although they can lead to an overall lower cost for the home, they can also bring on more financial hardship for the borrower. A financial emergency can make it hard to put together a large payment every two weeks. Having a single monthly payment can give the borrower some extra time to get together the money needed to pay the lender.

There are different loan terms for various types of mortgages. Most mortgages are set up to be repaid over thirty years. These are the mortgages that are most often discussed when interest rate averages are discussed in the news.

Fifteen-year mortgages are repaid faster. They often have a lower interest rate attached. The monthly payments are higher than for thirty-year mortgages. The tradeoff is that homebuyers end up paying less for their home because they aren't paying as much interest over a lengthy period of time.

Ten-year mortgages are an even lower total cost than the fifteen-year mortgage. Interest rates are lower, though monthly

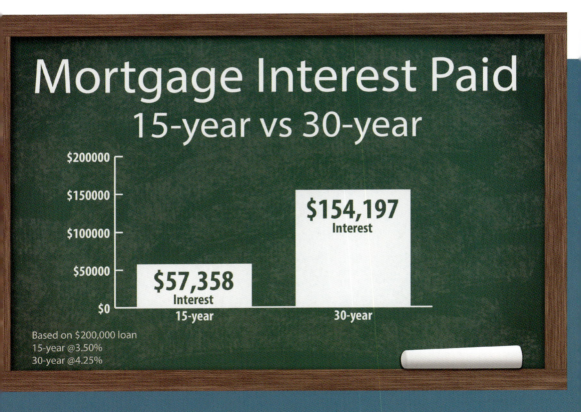

Borrowers who take out a fifteen-year mortgage could pay half as much in interest as those with thirty-year mortgages. However, their monthly payments will be much higher.

payments are much higher than for a more typical thirty-year mortgage. People who have a large amount of money saved up toward their home purchase and who feel confident that their employment situation will remain secure for several years might opt to take a ten-year mortgage.

Some people choose forty-year mortgages. These lengthy loans come with lower monthly payments, but the interest rates are often higher than with thirty-year or fifteen-year mortgages. People can sometimes buy a more expensive house than they would otherwise be able to afford with one of these loans, but the interest payments make it very costly to do so.

CHAPTER TWO

2 SOLID MORTGAGE FOUNDATIONS

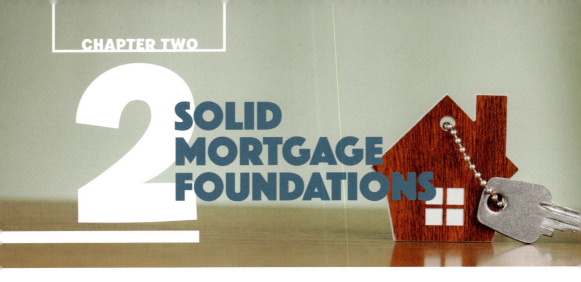

Applying for a mortgage is a major step for anyone looking to buy a home. The application process can take a long time to complete and can be intimidating for anyone who has never taken out a loan before. Someone with enough money saved for a down payment, a stable work situation, and a good credit history likely won't face too many challenges when it's time to apply.

CREDIT SCORES

Banks and other lenders look at a potential homebuyer's credit score before deciding to lend the individual money for a home. A credit score is a number that is intended to show how likely a person is to pay back money he or she has borrowed. Several factors go into a person's credit score. They include outstanding debts, late payments, how long the person's oldest account has been open, the number of accounts open, and how much money can be borrowed at that given time without going over credit card limits. Having a credit card bill go overdue can bring a credit score down, for example.

Credit scores are measured on a scale from 300 to 850 points. According to the credit bureau Equifax, a score over 700 is typically considered good. Scores over 800 are excellent. Those between 580 and 669 are fair. To be considered a low-risk or acceptable buyer by a lender, a person should have a credit

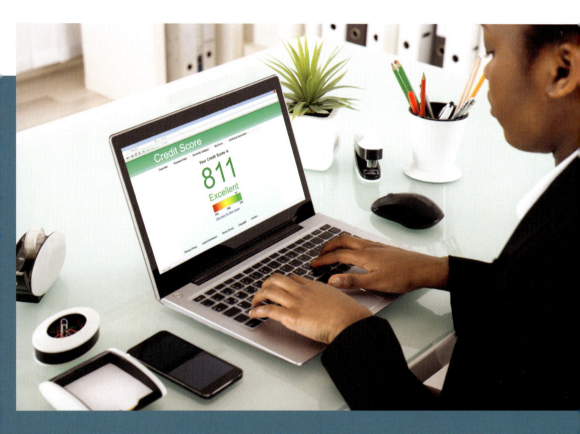

Having a high credit score makes it easier to borrow money at lower interest rates. Lenders often offer better rates on mortgages to people with very good or excellent scores.

score of at least 670. People can get their credit scores checked through one of the three major credit bureaus—TransUnion, Experian, and Equifax. Banks, lenders, and credit card companies also sometimes provide credit scores for their customers.

Having an acceptable credit score makes it easier to get a mortgage. People who have low credit scores can take steps to raise them, such as making payments on time, limiting the number of credit cards they apply for, paying debts quickly, and keeping card balances low.

THE DOWN PAYMENT QUESTION

A down payment represents the amount of money a homebuyer is comfortable paying without borrowing money. The more money a borrower is willing to pay up front, the more likely he or she is to be approved for a mortgage. A higher down payment also means that less money will have to be borrowed. People with lower credit scores may find it easier to get approved for a mortgage if they can make a large down payment.

It's not easy to decide how much to offer as a down payment. A homebuyer should be realistic about how much money he or she has saved and set aside enough to get through an emergency. Figuring out the monthly budget, earnings, and any unexpected expenses should all be part of the decision.

INCOME BALANCING ACT

Calculating a monthly budget requires an ability to be realistic about one's financial needs and ability to be disciplined in one's spending habits. A homebuyer needs to figure out how much he or she spends, and how much is left out of their monthly income. Spending calculations should be detailed.

A household budget should include earnings and estimates of regular expenses per month. Showing where the money goes makes it easier to spot opportunities to cut back on spending.

Even seemingly insignificant expenses such as haircuts should be included in the monthly budget.

A monthly budget should start with known expenses, such as rent, insurance costs, calling plans, or car payments. These are expenses that are likely to remain the same month after month. Regular expenses that may vary slightly should come next. These may include bills for utilities such as electricity, water, and gas. The month-to-month costs will likely vary slightly, but they'll probably be close enough that one can plan for them with a fair amount of accuracy.

Transportation costs can be harder to estimate accurately and fit into a budget. People who have to drive to a job will have more difficulty calculating their travel expenses than those who can take public transit, walk, or bike to work. Fuel costs can rise or fall from one day to the next. People also have to cover maintenance expenses, registration fees, vehicle insurance costs, and possibly tolls.

Lenders will want to know how much money a potential borrower makes and how much he or she can expect to make. This amount is weighed against existing debts. When getting ready to apply for a mortgage, it's important to track earnings and any debt payments made. Lenders will want to see pay stubs for people who work directly for an employer.

Contract employees who are hired for specific jobs with a company and are not on the regular employee payroll may have to show past tax forms as their proof of income. Still, it might be difficult for contract employees to get a mortgage. Lenders want evidence of an ability to bring in a steady income. Contract employees always face the risk that their clients will decide against hiring them again, even after they have demonstrated an ability to do the work required. Lenders sometimes want additional guarantees that these borrowers will be able to follow the terms of the mortgage.

Part-time employees might also encounter problems borrowing if they earn below a certain amount per month. Those who work two part-time jobs face the same situation. A lender may consider them to be too much of a risk because their employment situation is not stable.

People who own their own business can also experience difficulties securing a mortgage. They face many of the same

Some small business owners have trouble getting mortgages because of the seasonal nature of their goods or services unless they show that they have a steady flow of income.

SOLID MORTGAGE FOUNDATIONS

difficulties as contract employees. A lender might view their income as not stable, at least until they have become well-established in their field or industry. The type of business they have can also matter. A person who opens a housekeeping service or salon that sees a steady stream of clients and quickly shows a healthy profit is likely to have an easier time getting a mortgage than someone who opens a store that caters to a very specific type of customer.

YOUR FRIENDLY FINANCIAL ADVISER

Financial advisers are professionals who are qualified to provide advice to their clients on how to manage their assets to the greatest advantage. They can provide recommendations on investments, retirement planning, budgeting, and major purchases. Financial advisers can help homebuyers navigate the mortgage options that are available to them and decide what options are best.

Financial advisers are great at helping people make long-term plans and set goals far into the future. They can help homebuyers prepare for making a purchase by working with them to decide how much they can reasonably spend on a down payment and on monthly payments. If a homebuyer's credit score is low or he or she has trouble building savings, the financial adviser can make recommendations for ways to cut down on spending and improve the person's credit. Financial advisers charge fees, but the assistance they provide can save homebuyers a great deal of money.

Applicants for a mortgage will want to make sure they have all of their earnings accounted for. This total should include any outside income that comes from doing contract work apart from their full-time job. If they have a part-time job in addition to their full-time job, that will have to be included. Income from stock market investments, rental properties, savings accounts, and other sources should be part of the calculations.

PREQUALIFYING PREPARATION

Mortgage lenders often ask potential borrowers to go through a prequalification process. Prequalification can help banks and other lending institutions decide whether a potential borrower has the financial security to take out a loan. The process can tell the potential borrower the size of the mortgage he or she can reasonably expect to receive.

Prequalifying consists of answering a series of questions. These include the person's total earnings, with the money that person takes home from a job, the individual's investments, and other sources given as one sum. He or she will also answer questions about employment and work history. The questionnaire may ask how long the person has been at his or her current job, for example, or how long he or she has been employed.

Financial history questions can include the individual's current debts, such as a car loan, and whether the person has ever had to file for bankruptcy. Bankruptcy refers to the state of being bankrupt, or having more debts than total assets and being unlikely to be able to pay off those debts. Someone

A credit history questionnaire helps lenders understand a person's financial situation. The responses can tell the lender whether the mortgage applicant is likely to repay the loan.

declared bankruptcy could be considered a major financial risk and would be very unlikely to be able to get a mortgage under most circumstances.

Prequalification questions also include the person's credit score. Having a strong credit score in the excellent or very good categories can help increase the size of the mortgage loan a person is likely to be able to prequalify to get. When taken along with strong annual earnings and a lack of existing debt, a strong credit score can help a person secure a sizable prequalifying mortgage estimate.

There are things that a person can do to get ready for the prequalifying process. Some companies who are not connected to actual lenders may offer access to online tools that simulate the prequalification process. Users can enter their information just as they would do in an actual prequalifying questionnaire and then they can see how much of a loan they are likely to qualify for.

Paying down existing debts before prequalifying can help. So can taking another job at the same workplace that comes with higher pay. However, leaving one's employer for another that pays more might give the impression that the borrower lacks professional stability.

People who indicate through the prequalification process that they meet the lender's requirements will receive a prequalification letter. This letter will state the amount that the lender would be willing to lend. The prequalifying letter can send a signal to lenders that the homebuyer is serious about borrowing and is prepared to take this important step toward purchasing a home.

MYTHS & FACTS

MYTH **Homebuyers need perfect credit ratings to get a mortgage.**

Fact *There are mortgage options available that can help people who have credit scores as low as 600 purchase a home.*

MYTH **A person's income is the most important factor when applying for a mortgage.**

Fact *Regardless of income, the amount of debt a person carries affects the size of the mortgage he or she can get.*

MYTH **Prequalifying for a mortgage guarantees that a person will be able to buy a house.**

Fact *Lenders and sellers place a greater emphasis on preapproval, which is a similar process requiring that the homebuyer submit documentation proving his or her income, credit score, and other information.*

CHAPTER THREE

3 A PERFECT MORTGAGE FIT

There are many places to go to get a mortgage, and it can be tricky for a homebuyer to choose the right option. Many people go to a bank for their mortgage. Others turn to lenders who specialize in mortgage loans. The US government also provides some mortgage services. These services can help people with lower incomes, farmers, and military personnel and veterans realize their dreams of homeownership.

With so many choices available, it may seem that it wouldn't make a difference which option a homebuyer chooses. That isn't the case. Not every lender is right for every borrower. Some may offer great interest rates that seem too good to be true. Others might see a would-be borrower as totally unfit for a loan, when that isn't actually the case. It's vital that a person thinking about taking a mortgage research the options thoroughly so that he or she can make the best, most informed decision possible.

COMPARISON SHOPPING

There are two basic options for finding a mortgage: direct lenders and mortgage brokers. Direct lenders include banks, credit unions, nonbank lenders, and mortgage banks. Mortgage brokers act as intermediaries between borrowers and many different lenders. They work to connect borrowers with the best mortgage options available for each individual.

Banks are a common place to go for a mortgage. Many people who already have an account at a bank may then be

Mortgage brokers work with people to help them get the best mortgage possible to match their financial situation and the type of home they want to buy.

WHAT YOU NEED TO KNOW ABOUT MORTGAGES

familiar with their mortgage offerings. In some cases, banks can be relatively easy for people seeking a mortgage to deal with. The bank already has access to a person's account balances. Some banks might offer better loan terms or interest rates to their account holders.

Getting a mortgage from a bank offers several distinct advantages over other institutions. Borrowers who have their mortgage through a bank can always go to their local branch if there's some kind of problem with their loan. Sometimes banks have standing preapproval offers for their clients. This preapproval offer makes the process of applying for a mortgage much simpler.

Banks also offer a variety of convenient services to their clients. It can be simpler to go to one place for a checking account, savings account, and mortgage. Other financial products can also be advantageous to mortgage borrowers. Banks can offer a line of home equity credit that can be very useful to borrowers once they've completed their home purchase. Home equity loans or credit accounts can be used to cover mortgage insurance costs or to help make a down payment. Once you're in the home, this credit can be used to make improvements, such as major repairs, additions, or remodeling projects. A bank that a borrower already has a solid relationship with may be more willing to extend those services.

The relationship a borrower has with his or her bank can also have a positive impact on some mortgage expenses. Fees and closing costs might be lower. The personal and hands-on aspect of taking a mortgage from a bank is also

Freddie Mac and Fannie Mae play a large role in stabilizing the mortgage market and in keeping the cost of mortgages down for millions of borrowers.

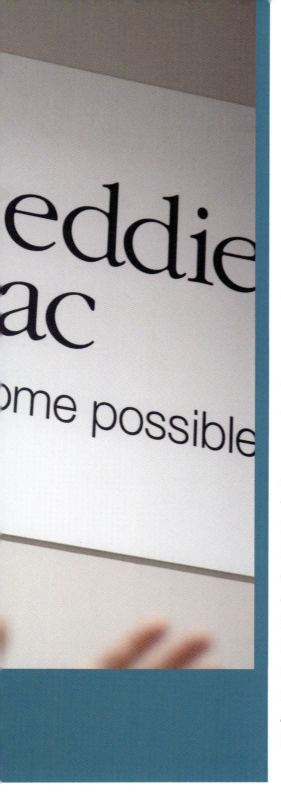

important. Borrowers can get to know their mortgage officers at a bank, and those employees can help them understand the process and work through any problems in face-to-face meetings.

Credit unions operate in a way that's similar to how banks work. They can help borrowers get home equity loans and lines of credit. Their financial services are all easily accessible in one place, and borrowers can arrange to meet with their mortgage officers. There are advantages that credit unions have over banks. Sometimes the cost of borrowing can be lower with credit unions. Banks don't control the rate at which a homebuyer borrows his or her mortgage because banks usually sell those loans. The mortgage rates set by banks are generally established by the two major national

A PERFECT MORTGAGE FIT

mortgage lenders, the Federal National Mortgage Association (FNMA, also known as Fannie Mae) and Freddie Mac. Credit unions keep their mortgages in-house. They may offer their members slightly lower rates on mortgages than those given by the national lenders. Credit unions may be able to make these offers because they are nonprofit entities, unlike banks. A credit union's owners are its members.

Banks typically sell their mortgages to one of the big national lenders, either Fannie Mae or Freddie Mac. Credit unions do not sell mortgages. Their focus is on using the interest earned from mortgages and other loans as income. Banks instead might sell their loans for a flat fee. When a mortgage loan is sold, the borrower is informed and has to begin making payments to the new institution now holding the loan. Sometimes the shift can be sudden and a borrower might be late in making a payment. Homebuyers who have an escrow account may encounter problems because of this change as well.

Mortgage banks are financial companies that focus strictly on mortgage lending. Banks and credit unions may lend money to their customers to purchase a car, cover medical bills, or pay other major expenses. Mortgage banks don't lend money for any other purpose than buying a home. Online lenders also provide mortgages. They work in much the same way as mortgage banks, although the entire transaction takes place online.

Mortgage brokers are the alternative to the direct lenders like banks, credit unions, and mortgage banks. Mortgage brokers represent many lenders at once. These lenders send the mortgage brokers rate sheets that list all of their financial products—the various types of mortgages they're offering, the rates, and what a borrower needs to do to qualify.

Mortgage brokers can help homebuyers find the best financial products for their specific circumstances. They often have more options available to them than banks or credit unions, which may offer only a handful of different mortgage types. Because they work with many different types of lenders,

FEDERAL PROGRAMS

Private banks, credit unions, and mortgage lenders aren't the only places homebuyers can look for mortgages. There are several options provided by the federal government to people who meet certain qualifications. First-time homebuyers can apply for a Federal Housing Administration (FHA) loan. These mortgages typically carry lower interest rates and are intended to help people with lower credit ratings and those who can't make a large down payment.

Fannie Mae and Freddie Mac also offer low-interest mortgages to first-time homebuyers who have good credit but little money saved. They typically require a 3 percent down payment.

The US Department of Agriculture guarantees some mortgages for lower-income homebuyers who are purchasing properties in rural areas. The US Department of Veterans Affairs provides housing loans for current military personnel, veterans, and their families.

mortgage brokers might be able to find more favorable rates or terms than a bank or credit union.

Comparison shopping for the right mortgage can be easier for homebuyers who go to a mortgage broker. The borrower has to visit several direct lenders to learn about all the different types of mortgages available and find the most favorable terms. Mortgage brokers can provide that information easily and in one place.

A PREAPPROVAL PROCESS

Once a homebuyer decides which lender to choose, it's time to meet and discuss budgeting and finances. Whether the borrower chooses a direct lender or a mortgage broker, the lender will make recommendations based on several factors. Income, debts, and financial history will be discussed, as well as the general price range of the type of home that the borrower wants to purchase.

Homebuyers often get prequalified for a mortgage to see how much they would likely be eligible to borrow. Prequalification gives the homebuyer an idea of what he or she could reasonably expect to borrow based on the state of the homebuyer's finances at that time. Homebuyers can take that information and attempt to improve the amount they could borrow by becoming more disciplined in their spending and paying down debts.

Prequalification questionnaires only scratch the surface, however. The borrower fills in all of the information, and there isn't any in-depth investigation on the part of a lender to prove that the data submitted is accurate.

Once the homebuyer is ready to commit to purchasing a home and has chosen a lender, he or she should go to that lender for a mortgage preapproval. A preapproval is somewhat similar to a prequalification. In both instances, the borrower submits financial information to the lender. One big difference is that during the preapproval process the lender checks to make sure that all of the information the borrower has submitted is accurate.

PROVIDING PROOF

The borrower fills out a full preapproval application that the lender will send to the underwriter, which is the bank, investment house, or insurer that guarantees the loan. The questions include information such as where the applicant works, how long he or she has been there, and how much he or she earns in salary or hourly wages. Some lenders require borrowers to submit documents to prove what they report. The borrower might have to turn over tax returns, bank statements showing how much he or she has saved, and documents to prove their employment, such as pay stubs. The lender may contact the borrower's employer to confirm information such as length of employment.

Typically, a person who is looking to be preapproved for a mortgage should be prepared to show two years of tax forms, proof of current income, and proof of income to date for the year. Proof of other sources of income besides job earnings should also be included. These sources might include profits from online sales or contract work done on

When meeting with a bank loan officer, borrowers may need to bring important documents with them such as bank statements, tax forms, or pay stubs.

the side, or part-time earnings from a second job. Bank statements serve as proof of assets and include any savings accounts or investments that can be turned into cash. These demonstrate that the borrower has the funds to cover a down payment, closing costs, and fees.

During prequalification, a borrower can enter an estimate of his or her credit score. For preapproval, the lender contacts the credit-reporting bureaus to obtain the borrower's credit score at that time. The lender will need the borrower's personal identification to get the credit report. This information includes his or her Social Security number and driver's license or other government-issued photo identification. The credit score gives the lender an idea of the borrower's past record of paying debts and likelihood of repaying the mortgage. Many lenders require a credit score of at least 620, according to the FHA.

This chart shows credit score ranges and how lenders typically categorize them. People with FICO scores in the "Poor" or "Very Poor" ranges often have a hard time borrowing money.

A PERFECT MORTGAGE FIT

Some FHA loans that are typically reserved for people who are low earners may require a score that high. The lowest interest rates are often reserved for borrowers who have credit scores judged by the data analytics company Fair Isaac Corporation (FICO) to be in the range of 760 to 850. People with lower scores likely will be required to make a higher down payment.

After the application is submitted, the underwriter issues one of four decisions: approved; approved with conditions; suspended (more information is needed); and denied. Approved mortgages set forth the amount that the lender is loaning to the homebuyer, the interest rate the homebuyer can expect to pay, and the term of the loan. Penalties for making late payments and other conditions might be included in the approval.

Some homebuyers are preapproved with conditions. These conditions may be that the buyer pays off a loan or agrees to sell his or her current home before closing on the mortgage. Sometimes additional documents are needed to show proof of income. In other cases, the borrower may have to make a higher down payment than usual to get a mortgage to secure a lower monthly payment amount. When a borrower is preapproved with conditions, the mortgage paperwork will often be completed and ready to go once the conditions have been met.

Some preapproval applications are suspended. This case often happens when the borrower has failed to provide enough documentation. He or she may be missing bank statements or proof of income. The application is put on hold until these documents can be provided.

Not every preapproval application ends well. Mortgage underwriters sometimes decide to deny an application. It means that the mortgage underwriter has analyzed the applicant's earnings, debts, and assets and determined that there is too much risk that the mortgage will not be repaid.

Although a denial is definitely negative, it doesn't mean that the applicant will never get a mortgage. A good loan officer will be able to tell applicants if there are factors that could result in them being denied, such as not enough income or too many outstanding debts. The loan officer should keep the borrower informed of these situations throughout the process so that a denial is not a complete surprise. The lender can give the denied applicant the reasons for the denial. The applicant can then work on correcting any problems so that he or she can be approved the next time. This action could mean taking care of outstanding debts or working to raise the individual's credit score.

Homebuyers who are denied can also try shopping around for different lenders. Some banks or mortgage lenders may be more willing to work with people who have lower incomes or more debt. A mortgage broker can often help find the right lender to grant preapproval based on the borrower's financial circumstances. A borrower can fill out preapproval applications with multiple lenders at the same time. There's no obligation on the borrower's part to accept a preapproval from any lender.

CHAPTER FOUR

4 CLOSING TIME

With a preapproval letter in hand, the borrower can move forward with purchasing his or her new home in a good position to receive the mortgage loan he or she needs. Many people hire a real estate agent to help them find the right home and navigate the purchasing process.

MAKING A COMMITMENT

Once the preapproval letter is issued, the lender gives the buyer a loan commitment verifying the value of the property and the borrower's financial information. The full mortgage application then goes to an underwriter, which is the financial institution that actually covers the cost of the mortgage.

When the borrower finally has a mortgage approved, the final loan documents have to be certified. This step can be done by a notary public or an escrow agent. Notary publics are officials who are appointed by a state government to serve as impartial witnesses when documents need to be signed, such as mortgages and deeds. Some real estate agents and loan officers are also notary publics and can serve as the witness.

Their signature guarantees that the financial commitment was made without any fraud or deceptions on the part of any of the parties involved.

The preapproved borrower gets a letter from the lender. The letter includes a conditional commitment to making a loan of a certain amount within a certain time period. In many cases, this preapproval commitment is good for sixty days or ninety

Once a mortgage approval is formally notarized, the document demonstrates to sellers that the potential homebuyer has the financial means to make the purchase.

CLOSING TIME

days. It may also include an interest rate estimate, indicating how much the borrower can expect to pay in interest.

Loan officers or brokers take the completed applications and any required material such as tax return documents and submit them to an automated system. The system calculates whether the borrower can be preapproved. It also determines the size of the loan for which he or she can be preapproved.

The preapproval letter can serve as proof that the homebuyer has the financial means to make a down payment and cover closing costs and other expenses. It's proof they have the financial backing of a bank or lender. It offers a guarantee to the seller that the final sale price will be paid.

Because the preapproval letter sets a time limit and expires after a certain period, the borrower has to be ready to start seriously looking for a home when the letter arrives. Many preapproval letters expire after sixty to ninety days. By having a preapproval letter, borrowers can show sellers that they are committed to purchasing a home and have the resources to complete the deal.

THE CLOSING TABLE

Borrowers who have a preapproval letter can enter the housing market to look for their dream home. They may already know what they want to buy or they may still be searching for the right fit. When they're ready to make a purchase, several things have to happen to satisfy the lender that the home is a good investment.

In many places, a home inspection is required before a home can be sold. Inspectors who are licensed by the city, county, or state government go through the home to make sure it meets building codes and is safe to inhabit.

The home inspection includes a close examination of the building's interior and exterior. The inspector looks at plumbing, wiring, the foundations, the walls, and the roof. The inspector checks for building code violations, such as porches that don't meet local standards. Any problems with the building are included in a report. These could range from a sinking foundation to an illegally installed bathroom that needs to be removed. In some cases, the mortgage lender will require the seller to make any changes that are necessary for the home to pass

Before the sale of a home is finalized, a home inspector evaluates the physical structure and interior systems, such as plumbing and electrical wiring.

another inspection. Otherwise, the lender won't approve a mortgage and the seller will have to find another buyer.

The home inspection is one way lenders protect the investments they make when issuing mortgages. Lenders also have professional appraisers compare the house, condo, or co-op unit to others that are located nearby. These comparisons let the lender know what the typical market price is for similar homes and whether the seller is asking a fair price. Appraisers also check current home prices throughout the housing market in the area and look at the information from the home inspection. The appraiser gathers all of that information and uses it to decide on a value for the home. The value may be higher, lower, or nearly equal to the price that the seller has set. Sellers may have their own appraisal performed.

A home appraisal can protect homebuyers from overpaying and assure banks that they aren't lending borrowers more money than the home is worth.

CLOSING TIME

Different appraisers may come up with very different values for a home. An inspection can turn up major problems, including issues that the seller did not know about. All of that information is brought to the negotiating table. The buyer and lender usually want to purchase the home at the lowest possible price, though they may have to raise their offer if there is a lot of competition for a home from other potential buyers. The negotiations may include agreements from the sellers that they will fix any issues before the sale is finalized. Issues that the sellers can't fix quickly can help bring the price

ONE-STOP SHOPS

Real estate agents seldom play a direct role in helping a homebuyer secure a mortgage. However, experienced agents often have professional connections to mortgage brokers and other professionals who can help homebuyers make good decisions. Some real estate brokerages have experts in several related fields on staff and can offer a one-stop shop to homebuyers.

These experts often include appraisers who can provide an accurate estimate of a home's value. Their reports can help the homebuyer secure a lower price at the negotiation table. Mortgage brokers may also be part of a real estate office. They can work with potential homebuyers who have not applied for preapproval, or they may be able to offer more money or a better rate than the homebuyers have found elsewhere.

down, if the lender is still willing to back a mortgage for a home with defects.

Lenders may also require a title search. This process involves an investigation of the property and the title granting ownership through public records. The title search is intended to turn up any questions of ownership or potential legal snags, such as back taxes or liens (the use of the property to gain credit to cover a debt) that could complicate the purchase. Title searches can be carried out by professional investigators or by the purchaser.

FOLLOWING THROUGH

With the loan documents, the borrower has committed to paying the purchase cost of the home, including the down payment, any closing costs or fees associated with the purchase, and mortgage payments. In most cases, the borrower will have to make these payments once per month for at least ten years, and possibly as long as forty-five years.

Mortgage payments go to the lender. Part of each payment goes toward paying the principal. The rest goes toward paying the interest costs. Often, the largest portion of each payment is on interest. The borrower can cut down the amount of interest that he or she actually has to pay by paying extra every month, or by making an extra payment each year.

Borrowers must be prepared to make at least the agreed-upon payment on time every month. Failing to do so can lead to the lender adding penalties for late payments. Paying extra early on does not mean that the borrower can skip payments later on or make partial payments. He or she is still responsible for the agreed-upon monthly amount. Penalties from late payments can pile up and drastically increase the cost of the home.

In some cases, the lender may be willing to work with the borrower if an unexpected financial hardship comes up that makes it too challenging to meet the minimum payment. The borrower may be able to negotiate a lower payment over a longer term. The borrower has to do this negotiation while working with the lender, however. Otherwise the penalties will continue to accumulate. Late payments that are thirty days past due are reported to the credit bureaus. This occurrence can lead to a lower credit rating for the borrower. Lenders eventually send a letter of default to formally inform the borrower that he or she is past due in making a payment. Many lenders send these notices between thirty days and sixty days after a missed payment.

Sometimes lenders hire debt collection agencies to call the borrower about past-due payments. Borrowers receiving calls from collection agencies can often work with the lender to get back on track. A borrower who is willing to take responsibility for past-due mortgage debt by letting the lender know when he or she can get the account current can avoid the worst outcomes.

People who fall behind on their mortgage payments may be offered a chance to pay the full amount that they've missed in a single sum. This situation is called reinstatement. If the borrower can't come up with the money to cover the

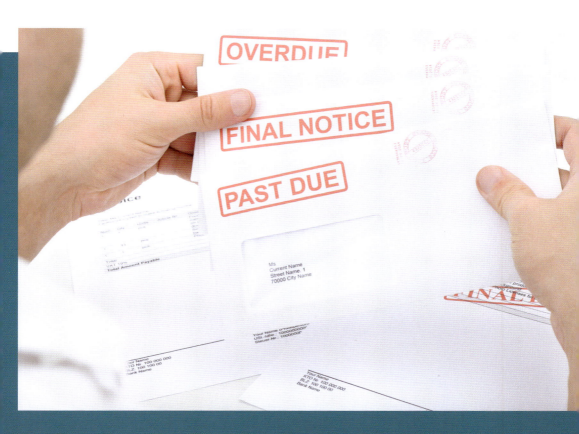

Missing mortgage payments can have serious financial consequences, such as incurring late fees, damaging a borrower's credit score, or even leading to an owner losing a home.

payments they've missed at one time, the lender can give them the option to spread out the payments over an extended period of time. This agreement is called forbearance.

In a worst-case scenario, a borrower who falls way behind on payments could face threats of foreclosure. A foreclosure happens when the lender seeks to end the loan agreement and take full possession of the property. In some cases,

When a home is foreclosed, anyone living there has to move out as the lender takes possession. Foreclosed homes may look abandoned and unwelcoming from the outside.

foreclosures are handled in courts. Other cases don't require a court hearing. The past-due notice represents the first step in the foreclosure process. If the borrower and the lender can't work out an arrangement to bring the loan current, the lender can file the appropriate paperwork to begin foreclosing on the home.

The borrower may still be able to work with the lender and stop the foreclosure through forbearance or reinstatement. If that's impossible, the lender ultimately takes control of the property and puts it up for sale.

A foreclosure can have a serious impact on a person's credit and finances. By keeping up with mortgage payments and being honest with the lender when those payments are hard to make, a borrower can avoid foreclosure and come closer every month to owning the home outright.

10 GREAT QUESTIONS
TO ASK A MORTGAGE BROKER

1. How can I improve my credit score?

2. How much money do I need to save to make a down payment on a home?

3. What kind of home can I afford to buy?

4. What mortgage terms are best for my financial circumstances?

5. Where can I go to find a lender who is willing to offer a lower interest rate?

6. Should I choose a fixed-rate or an adjustable-rate mortgage?

7. What steps can I take to be preapproved for a larger mortgage?

8. What happens when I am late making a mortgage payment?

9. Should I take out a second mortgage?

10. What happens after I finish paying off my mortgage?

CHAPTER FIVE

5 HOME FREE

Once a mortgage is paid off, ownership of the home is transferred from the loan underwriter to the borrower. By making payments on time, borrowers can finally call their house or condo their own. The process of paying off a mortgage takes many years and many thousands of dollars. By the time the mortgage is paid in full, it often represents the most expensive purchase the homebuyer has ever made.

REASONS FOR REFINANCING

A borrower's financial circumstances often change during the time that he or she is paying off a mortgage. The borrower may have more expenses, such as paying tuition for children. Borrowers

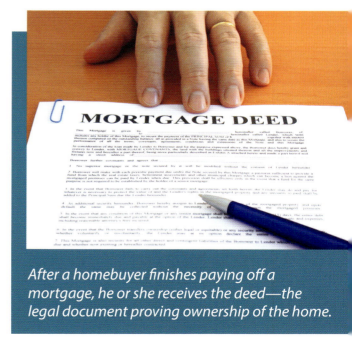

After a homebuyer finishes paying off a mortgage, he or she receives the deed—the legal document proving ownership of the home.

HOME FREE 55

who want to lower their monthly payments can work with their lender to get a more favorable interest rate and term. This process, called refinancing, basically means replacing the old mortgage with a new one. Refinancing can often lower monthly mortgage payments because the borrower is paying less on interest.

Borrowers refinance for many reasons. Sometimes a change in careers can lead to a person earning less money, at least in the short term. Major life events such as having children, getting a divorce, and going through a medical emergency can reduce the amount a person can comfortably pay on a mortgage.

Many mortgage lenders offer refinancing options to their borrowers. Refinancing is particularly useful to borrowers who have an adjustable interest rate. They can work with loan officers to convert their loan to a fixed-rate mortgage, which can lower their interest payments. Refinancing can also be helpful if the borrower's credit score has improved. He or she can likely qualify for a lower interest rate than the one initially attached to the mortgage. Changes in a home's value or in the market itself can also be good reasons to refinance. A borrower can make a solid argument for refinancing if the home's market value falls far below the purchase price.

Borrowers need to be ready to present evidence of changed circumstances to a loan officer. Supporting documents such as medical or tuition bills, tax returns, pay stubs, and property tax assessments can help the borrower build a case for a lower interest rate.

For some homeowners, refinancing a home can help achieve financial goals such as lowering monthly payments or qualifying for a better interest rate.

EARLY PAYMENT PAYOFFS

Borrowers can pay off a mortgage before the terms specified in the loan agreement by paying a little more than the minimum payment every month. Making slightly larger monthly payments lead to paying less interest later. This practice helps the borrower save money by lowering the total cost of the home. Paying the mortgage early can also improve a person's credit score, and getting ahead on payments might help the borrower refinance for a better interest rate.

There can be a downside to paying off a mortgage early. Some lenders charge a penalty for paying the debt ahead of schedule. These early payment fees can be costly, and might wipe out any money the borrower saves on interest. Lenders, particularly those that specialize in mortgages, see the interest payments a person makes as their profit. Paying off the mortgage early deprives them of their profits. Fees for early payment offset that loss. Any penalties for early payment should be included in the original mortgage document.

GETTING THE DEED

When the final mortgage payment is made, the borrower is informed by the lender that the mortgage is paid in full. Several documents are also released by the lender to the borrower. These documents make it possible for the borrower to get the deed to the property.

The canceled promissory note is the document that the borrower signed when taking out the mortgage, or signed later after refinancing. It's the document that states the borrower promises to make payments on time for the term of the mortgage. When the mortgage is paid off, it is sent back to the borrower. The lender marks it "cancelled" or "paid in full" before sending it to the borrower to show that the borrower has fulfilled his or her obligations.

A certificate of satisfaction is sent to the city, town, or county office where the deed to the property has been filed. It states that the borrower has met all of the requirements of the mortgage. This document notifies the local government that the deed to the home can be released to the borrower. It is filed among official documents to create a public record that the borrower has paid his or her mortgage debt.

Once the city or county has been informed of the satisfaction of the mortgage, the deed can be released to the borrower. The deed is the document that gives the borrower sole rights to the property and makes him or her responsible for it. With the deed, the borrower can decide to sell the home or use it as collateral for a loan.

OWNERSHIP RESPONSIBILITIES

With the mortgage paid off, important responsibilities fall to the homeowner that were taken care of by the lender. Mortgage lenders own the property until the homeowner can finish paying the mortgage. In that role, they have to cover a lot of extra expenses. Some of these expenses may come as a surprise to the homebuyer. However, they won't be nearly as costly as monthly mortgage payments.

Paying off a mortgage will give homeowners peace of mind and improve their financial security. Planning ahead can help buyers reduce the amount paid on interest.

Mortgage borrowers rarely have to worry about directly covering the cost of property taxes on their own. Lenders generally pay local property tax costs on the home. These taxes are usually assessed by county governments as a percentage of the value of a home. Improvements, the value of other homes, the number of bedrooms, and the size of the lot for houses are factors in determining the home's value and how much

A SECOND MORTGAGE

Some people take a second mortgage to cover expenses, such as renovation costs, while they're still paying down their original mortgage. A second mortgage is money borrowed that uses the amount the borrower has already paid on the mortgage (called equity) as collateral. Second mortgages often allow people to borrow a large amount of money at lower interest rates than other types of loans. People often use them to make big purchases or cover other debts.

There are risks to taking a second mortgage. There is a chance of foreclosure if something happens and the borrower can't make the payments on the second mortgage. Fees for these types of loans can be expensive, and the interest rates are often higher than for the first mortgage. Significantly, the second mortgage puts the borrower deeper in debt when he or she should be getting closer to paying off the first mortgage.

tax the owner has to pay. In some places, taxes are assessed twice each year. In other places, people pay only once annually.

Property taxes can also be dramatically different based on where the home is located. Taxes are often higher in cities and towns than in rural areas. People living in cities and towns usually pay more in property taxes to help cover the cost of the broader range of services available to them. Those living in rural areas may have to pay different rates based on whether their home is part of a farm and the number of outbuildings like barns or sheds that are situated on it.

Some mortgage lenders have their borrowers pay a little extra on their mortgages to help cover property taxes. Responsibility for paying property taxes becomes the homebuyer's once the mortgage is fully paid. It will be up to the homeowner to challenge tax assessments that he or she believes are too high in an effort to pay less.

People who purchase condos, co-op units, homes in gated communities, and houses in some subdivisions have to pay association fees in addition to their property taxes. This homeowners association (HOA) fee is usually a monthly charge that covers expenses such as upkeep and landscaping. Condo owners may pay toward utilities that are used by everyone in the building, such as electricity in public areas. Services such as snow removal, garbage pickup, and cleaning may also be covered. These expenses are covered by the borrower after the mortgage is paid.

Homeowners insurance policies will also have to be updated to show that the borrower is now the sole owner of the property. Homeowners insurance is not legally required, and a person who has finished paying off a mortgage may decide to cancel his or her policy. Doing so, however, could leave the person financially liable for accidents and natural disasters that happen on the property.

JOYS OF HOMEOWNERSHIP

There are many benefits to owning a home. A person who finishes paying off a mortgage and owns a home outright will not have to worry about having to make that monthly

Property tax bills may come as a shock for some new homeowners, but many factors can affect the rates set by state and local governments.

payment again. For borrowers still paying mortgages, that money is going toward a home they will eventually own outright. They aren't paying a landlord who could raise their rent or cause other problems. Once the mortgage is paid,

For many people, homeownership is part of attaining the American dream. It represents a sense of stability, financial security, and pride.

they won't have to worry about foreclosure. Homebuyers can look at the property they've purchased as an investment. By the time the mortgage has been paid off, its value may have increased dramatically. Owning a home also gives a person a sense of security. He or she always has a place to return to at the end of the day.

Owning a home is also a great responsibility. The homeowner has to take care of repairs, maintenance, and upkeep. It is also a great opportunity. Homeowners can take pride in owning a place they have made their own.

GLOSSARY

asset Money, property, or something of value that a person or company owns.

bankruptcy The inability to pay one's debts as they come due; having more debt than assets.

broker A professional whose job is to organize business transactions between two parties, such as home purchases or mortgage loans.

closing costs The expenses and fees charged during a real estate sale. These might include taxes, title insurance, escrow fees, lender fees, lawyer fees, points, appraisal fee, prepaid homeowners insurance, and so forth.

credit A person's ability to make a purchase with the understanding that he or she will pay for it later in a prearranged manner.

credit union A cooperative financial organization whose members can take loans from their combined savings.

debt Money owed by a person to a company, a business, or another person.

deed An official and legally binding document that is signed and sealed to transfer ownership of a property from one person to another.

default A person's failure to pay money he or she owes.

down payment The first payment when buying an item, with the rest of the amount to be paid later.

escrow Money, legal documents, or property held in an account to guarantee that certain conditions or obligations are met.

forbearance Holding back from taking legal action, such as enforcing debt payments.

foreclosure The process of taking control or ownership of a property when the purchaser fails to pay back the money borrowed to pay for it.

interest Money a borrower has to pay to an individual or institution that has made a loan to that person.

investment Something purchased that is expected to increase in value over time.

mortgage A legal agreement in which money is borrowed to purchase a home, then repaid over time on a monthly basis.

principal The amount of money borrowed without interest.

renovate To make repairs or improvements to something, such as a home.

tenant A person who rents a home or property from the person who owns it.

term The length of time that a legal, financial, or business agreement lasts.

underwriter A company or person who provides financial backing to cover a purchase.

FOR MORE INFORMATION

Canada Mortgage and Housing Corporation (CMHC)
700 Montreal Road
Ottawa, ON K1A 0P7
Canada
(613) 748-2000
Website: https://www.cmhc-schl.gc.ca
Facebook: @cmhc.schl
Instagram: @cmhc_schl
Twitter: @CMHC_ca
The Canada Mortgage and Housing Corporation serves as Canada's national housing agency, providing mortgage loan insurance and other resources for consumers and industry professionals.

Canadian Real Estate Association (CREA)
200 Catherine Street, 6th Floor
Ottawa, ON K2P 2K9
Canada
(613) 237-7111
Website: https://www.crea.ca
Facebook: @CREA.ACI
Instagram: @crea_aci
Twitter: @CREA_ACI
The Canadian Real Estate Association represents the interests of Canadian real estate brokers, agents, and salespeople.

Consumer Financial Protection Bureau
1700 G St. NW
Washington, DC 20552
(855) 411-2372
Website: https://www.consumerfinance.gov
Facebook and Twitter: @CFPB
The Consumer Finance Protection Bureau is a US government agency established to make sure borrowers are treated fairly by bankers and lenders. It gives people access to tools for reporting unfair lending practices and provides answers to common questions about borrowing.

Federal Home Loan Mortgage Corporation (FHLMC, also known as Freddie Mac)
Headquarters
8200 Jones Branch Drive
McLean, VA 22102-3110
(800) 424-5401
Website: http://www.freddiemac.com
Facebook and Twitter: @FreddieMac
Freddie Mac is a US government-backed enterprise that buys and sells mortgages in order to give buyers access to affordable mortgages.

Federal National Mortgage Association (FNMA, also known as Fannie Mae)
Headquarters
1100 15th Street, NW
Washington, DC 20005

FOR MORE INFORMATION

(800) 232-6643
Website: http://www.fanniemae.com
Facebook and Twitter: @FannieMae
Instagram: @officialfanniemae
Fannie Mae is a US government-backed enterprise that buys and sells mortgages in order to give buyers access to affordable mortgages. Fannie Mae buys from different sources and offers different programs than Freddie Mac.

Mortgage Bankers Association (MBA)
1919 M Street NW, 5th Floor
Washington, DC 20036
(800) 793-6222
Website: https://www.mba.org
Facebook and Twitter: @MBAMortgage
The Mortgage Bankers Association represents professionals in the real estate finance industry who provide mortgage loans.

National Association of Mortgage Brokers (NAMB)
601 Pennsylvania Avenue NW, South Building
Washington, DC 20004
(202) 434-8250
Website: https://www.namb.org
Twitter: @NAMBpros
The National Association of Mortgage Brokers represents professionals in the mortgage industry who help connect borrowers with mortgage providers.

National Association of Realtors (NAR)
430 North Michigan Avenue
Chicago, IL 60611
(800) 874-6500
Website: https://www.nar.realtor
Facebook and Twitter: @NARdotRealtor
Instagram: @realtors
Twitter: @nardotrealtor
The National Association of Realtors represents the interests of professionals in the real estate industry.

FOR FURTHER READING

Boneparth, Douglas A., and Heather Boneparth. *The Millennial Money Fix: What You Need to Know About Budgeting, Debt, and Finding Financial Freedom*. Wayne, NJ: Career Press, 2017.

Bray, Ilona M. *Nolo's Essential Guide to Buying Your First Home*, 6th ed. Berkeley, CA: Nolo, 2017.

Chalk, Dylan. *The Confident House Hunter: A Home Inspector's Tips for Finding Your Perfect House*. Springville, UT: Plain Sight Publishing, 2016.

Davidson, Liz. *What Your Financial Advisor Isn't Telling You: The 10 Essential Truths You Need to Know About Your Money*. Boston, MA: Houghton Mifflin Harcourt, 2016.

Doyle, Nancy. *Manage Your Financial Life: Just Starting Out*. Glencoe, IL: The Doyle Group, 2018.

Glink, Ilyce R. *100 Questions Every First-Time Home Buyer Should Ask—With Answers from Top Brokers from Around the Country*. 4th ed. New York, NY: Three Rivers Press, 2018.

McGuire, Kara. *Cover Your Assets: The Teens' Guide to Protecting Their Money and Their Stuff*. North Mankato, MN: Compass Point Books, 2015.

McGuire, Kara. *Smart Spending: The Teens' Guide to Cash, Credit, and Life's Costs*. North Mankato, MN: Compass Point Books, 2015.

Morrison, Jay. *Lord of My Land: 5 Steps to Homeownership*. Laveen, AZ: Good 2 Go Publishing, 2016.

Sherrod, Egypt. *Keep Calm ... It's Just Real Estate: Your No-Stress Guide to Buying A Home*. With Amber Noble Garland. Philadelphia, PA: Running Press, 2015.

Tyson, Eric. *Personal Finance in Your 20s for Dummies*. Hoboken, NJ: John Wiley & Sons, 2016.

Tyson, Eric, and Robert Griswold. *Mortgage Management for Dummies*. With Ray Brown. Hoboken, NJ: John Wiley & Sons, 2017.

Zschunke, Jeff. *I Didn't Learn That in High School: 199 Facts About Credit Scores*. Ocala, FL: Atlantic Publishing Group, 2017.

BIBLIOGRAPHY

Amadeo, Kimberly. "Freddie Mac, What It Does, Who Owns It, and How It Affects You." November 1, 2018. https://www.thebalance.com/what-is-freddie-mac-3305985.

Cornett, Brandon. "What Happens During the Foreclosure Process?" Home Buying Institute, 2018. http://www.homebuyinginstitute.com/mortgage/what-happens-during-the-foreclosure-process.

Frankel, Robin Saks. "What to Do When Your Mortgage Application Gets Denied." Bankrate, February 19, 2018. https://www.bankrate.com/finance/mortgages/mortgage-application-denied-dont-despair-1.aspx.

Freddie Mac. "30-Year Fixed-Rate Mortgages Since 1971." Retrieved March 13, 2019. http://www.freddiemac.com/pmms/pmms30.html.

Home Bay. "All About Escrow Fees: What They Are & Who Pays What." August 25, 2016. https://www.homebay.com/tips/all-about-escrow-fees-what-they-are-who-pays-what.

Kearns, Deborah. "Choosing Between an ARM Versus a Fixed-Rate Mortgage." Bankrate, December 5, 2018. https://www.bankrate.com/mortgages/arm-vs-fixed-rate.

Kearns, Deborah. "10 First-Time Homebuyer Grants and Programs." Bankrate, March 6, 2019. https://www.bankrate.com/mortgages/first-time-homebuyer-grants-and-programs.

Keefer, Amber. "Mortgage Approval with Conditions." The Nest. Retrieved March 6, 2019. https://budgeting.thenest.com/mortgage-approval-conditions-20251.html.

Kiplinger. "Home Prices in the 100 Largest Metro Areas." January 2019. https://www.kiplinger.com/tool/real-estate/T010-S003-home-prices-in-100-top-u-s-metro-areas/index.php.

Lewis, Marilyn. "Are 40-Year Mortgages Really a Thing?" NerdWallet, August 2, 2017. https://www.nerdwallet.com/blog/mortgages/are-40-year-mortgages-really-a-thing.

Martin, Emmie. "This Map Shows How Much More Expensive It Is to Own a Home Than to Rent in Every US State." CNBC, February 14, 2019. https://www.cnbc.com/2019/02/13/how-much-more-money-it-costs-to-own-a-home-than-rent-in-every-us-state.html?forYou=true.

McLean, Bethany. *Shaky Ground: The Strange Saga of the U.S. Mortgage Giants*. New York, NY: Columbia Global Reports, 2015.

Mercadante, Kevin. "Why You Should Get a Mortgage Through a Credit Union or Local Bank." Money Under 30, May 27, 2018. https://www.moneyunder30.com/why-you-should-get-a-mortgage-through-a-credit-union-or-local-bank.

Mitzsheva, Mack. "Can a Mortgage Company Have a Debt Collector Call if the Payment Is Not 30 Days Past Due?" SFGate. Retrieved March 6, 2019. https://homeguides.sfgate.com/can-mortgage-company

-debt-collector-call-payment-not-30-days-past-due-47862.html.

Montgomery, David. "Who Owns a Home in America, in 12 Charts." CityLab, August 8, 2018. https://www.citylab.com/life/2018/08/who-rents-their-home-heres-what-the-data-says/566933.

NOLO. "Should You Consult a Financial Advisor Before Buying a Home?" Retrieved March 6, 2019. https://www.nolo.com/legal-encyclopedia/should-consult-financial-adviser-before-buying-home.html.

Pogol, Gina. "Which Is Better? A Mortgage Broker or a Bank?" Mortgage Reports, January 21, 2019. https://themortgagereports.com/29656/who-is-better-a-mortgage-broker-or-a-bank.

Reed, David. *Mortgages 101: Quick Answers to Over 250 Critical Questions About Your Home Loan*. New York, NY: Anacom, 2018.

US Census Bureau. "Selected Housing Characteristics 2013–2017, American Community Survey 5-Year Estimates." 2017. https://factfinder.census.gov/faces/tableservices/jsf/pages/productview.xhtml?pid=ACS_17_5YR_DP04&src=pt.

Wachter, Susan M., and Marvin M. Smith, eds. *The American Mortgage System: Crisis and Reform*. Philadelphia, PA: University of Pennsylvania Press, 2011.

Whiteman, Doug. "Which Type of Mortgage Lender Is Right for You?" Bankrate, April 16, 2018. https://www.bankrate.com/finance/mortgages/which-type-of-lender-is-right-for-you--1.aspx.

INDEX

A

accidents, insurance coverage for, 10, 62
adjustable-rate mortgage (ARMs), 12, 54, 56
appraisal, 46, 48
approved application, 40
approved with conditions application, 40
assets, 24, 25, 38, 41
association fees, 62
automated preapproval system, 44

B

banks, as lenders, 30–32, 34
bank statements, 37, 38
biweekly mortgage payment, 15
blizzards, 10
borrowing limit, on credit cards, 18
budget, how to make one, 21–25
building code violations, 45
business owners, 23–24
buying, compared to renting, 13

C

canceled promissory note, 58–59
certificate of satisfaction, 59
cities, property tax rates in, 61
closing costs, 31, 44, 49
commitment letter, 43, 44
condominium, 4, 6, 7, 13, 55, 62
contract employees, 22–23
co-op, 13, 46, 62
credit cards, 15, 18–19, 20
credit score/history, 18–20, 24, 28, 38–39, 40, 50, 54, 56
credit unions, as lenders, 33–34

D

debt, 18, 20, 22, 25, 26, 27, 28, 36, 39, 41, 49, 50, 58, 59, 61
debt collection agencies, 50
deed, 59
defaulting, 15, 50
denied application, 40, 41
direct lenders, 29–30
down payment, determining, 20
driver's license, 39

E

early payments, 58
earthquakes, 10
Equifax, 19, 20
equity, 61
escrow account, 12, 34
escrow agent, 42
Experian, 20

F

Fair Isaac Corporation (FICO), 40
farmers, government mortgages for, 5

Federal Home Loan Mortgage Corporation (Freddie Mac), 10, 34, 35
Federal Housing Administration (FHA), 11, 35, 39, 40
federal loan programs, types of, 35
Federal National Mortgage Association (Fannie Mae), 34, 35
fifteen-year mortgages, 16
financial advisers, what they do, 24
fires, 10
fixed-rate mortgage, 12, 56
forbearance, 51
foreclosure, 51, 53, 61, 65
forty-year mortgage, 17

G

gated communities, fees for living in, 62

H

home equity loans, 31
home inspection, 45–46, 48
homeowners association (HOA), 62
homeowners insurance, 10, 62
home value, estimating, 42, 46, 48, 56, 60, 65
housing prices, average in United States, 4, 7

I

interest rate, 4, 10, 12, 15–17, 29, 31, 34, 35, 40, 44, 49, 54, 56, 58, 61

K

known expenses, 22

L

landscaping, 62
landslides, 10
low-income buyers, government mortgages for, 5, 11, 29, 35, 40
low-risk buyer, 19

M

market price, 46
monthly mortgage payment, 15
mortgage banks, 34
mortgage brokers, how they work, 29, 30, 34–36
mortgages
 components of, 9–12
 explanation of how they work, 4
 myths and facts about, 28

N

natural disasters, 10, 62
notary public, 42

P

part-time employees, 23
past-due payments/notices, 50, 53
pay stubs, 22, 37, 56
penalties, 49–50, 58
preapproval process, 37–41, 48
prequalifying, 25–27, 28, 36–37
principal, 9, 49

private mortgage insurance (PMI), 11
proof of employment/income, 22, 37, 40, 41
property taxes, 12, 13–14, 60–62

Q

questionnaires, for prequalification, 25, 27, 36

R

real estate offices, types of professionals employed by, 48
refinancing, 55–57
reinstatement, 50
renting, compared to buying, 13
risk, assessing for borrowers, 15
rural areas, property tax rates in, 61

S

second mortgage, 54, 61
Social Security number, 39
subdivisions, fees for living in, 62
suspended application, 40

T

tax returns, 37, 44, 56
ten-year mortgages, 16–17
term, 15
thirty-year mortgages, 15, 17
title search, 49
tornadoes, 10
TransUnion, 20

U

underwriter, 37, 40, 41, 42, 55
US Department of Agriculture, 11, 35
US Department of Veterans Affairs, 35
utilities, fees for, 62

V

veterans, government mortgages for, 5, 35

ABOUT THE AUTHOR

Jason Porterfield is an author and journalist living in Chicago, Illinois. He has written many books for young adults. These include works on financial topics such as *How a Recession Affects You* and *How a Depression Works*. He writes about real estate for several publications covering housing markets in Atlanta, Georgia; Boston, Massachusetts; Chicago, Illinois; Houston, Texas; and Miami, Florida, and has interviewed numerous mortgage brokers about their work.

PHOTO CREDITS

Cover Hisham Ibrahim/Getty Images; pp. 5, 23 Dragon Images/Shutterstock.com; pp. 7, 18, 29, 42, 55 (top) inxti/Shutterstock.com; p. 8 Ken Mellott/Shutterstock.com; p. 9 JohnKwan/Shutterstock.com; p. 11 © iStockphoto.com/maxexphoto; p. 14 fotog/Getty Images; p. 16 Karen Roach/Shutterstock.com; pp. 19, 46-47, 51 Andrey_Popov/Shutterstock.com; p. 21 Anatolii Mazhora/Shutterstock.com; p. 26 Rawpixel.com/Shutterstock.com; p. 30 fizkes/Shutterstock.com; pp. 32–33 Bloomberg/Getty Images; p. 38 goodluz/Shutterstock.com; p. 39 designmaestro/Shutterstock.com; p. 43 © iStockphoto.com/Tamarabegucheva; p. 45 fstop123/iStock/Getty Images; p. 52 rSnapshotPhotos/Shutterstock.com; p. 55 (bottom) marlee/Shutterstock.com; p. 57 Image Source/DigitalVision/Getty Images; p. 60 Ben Gingell/Shutterstock.com; p. 63 Lazar Unlimited/Shutterstock.com; p. 64 ImagesBazaar/Getty Images.

Design and Layout: Jennifer Moy; Editors: Kathy Kuhtz Campbell and Wendy Wong; Photo Researcher: Sherri Jackson